A Boy an

The Children's Relaxation Book

By Lori Lite
Illustrated by
M. Hartigan

Specialty Press, Inc.
Florida

Library of Congress Cataloging-in-Publication Data

Lite, Lori, 1961-
 A boy and a bear : the children's relaxation book / by Lori Lite :
 illustrated by M. Hartigan.
    p.   cm.
 Summary: A boy and a polar bear who share a friendship learn to
 relax together.
 ISBN 1-886941-07-6 (pbk.)
 [1. Relaxation — Fiction.   2. Polar bear — Fiction.   3. Bears — Fiction.]
 I. Hartigan, M., ill.
 PZ7.L6975Ba   1996
[E] — dc20   96-33818
                                                        CIP
                                                        AC

Published by Specialty Press, Inc.
300 N.W. 70th Avenue, Suite 102
Plantation, Florida 33317
(954) 792-8100

Second Printing, 1998

Manufactured in the United States of America

I dedicate this book to Tarin, Austin

and all the children of the world

who are the sparks of my creativity.

I thank God for walking me down

this path of helping children, and

my parents for teaching me to

touch the stars... Lori Lite

Congratulations!

You have taken a wonderful step in bringing relaxation to your child. This book teaches a simple breathing technique called circular breathing. I encourage you to read this book frequently to your child, even on a daily or nightly basis. You'll find that with repeated use your child will settle down to sleep more peacefully. Both you and your child will experience inner peace, calmness, and well being.

Once your child is familiar with this breathing technique try applying it outside of your home. Try it on the way to school, when your child is overstimulated, or when your child is angry. Your child will like the way it feels when he calms down and regains control of himself. Your child will be able to use this self-calming technique even when you're not around.

This story changed my life and the lives of my children. I hope it does the same for you and your child.

Look for my next book in this relaxation series, The Affirmation Web. This book will introduce your child to the world of affirmations. It is a delightful compliment to A Boy and a Bear.

Lori Lite

*One day a boy decided to climb a high
mountain covered with snow.*

A polar bear who lived on the other side of the mountain also decided to climb the mountain.

The boy worked very hard lifting his legs out of the deep snow.

So did the bear.

Step after step they both did climb...

until they were both very tired and glad to see a rock to rest on.

The boy jumped up on the rock and stamped the snow off his boots. He removed his back pack and was startled by two dark eyes looking at him.

Feeling brave and friendly, the boy said, "Hi! This is a great rock to rest on. Why don't you join me?" The bear smiled and climbed up onto the rock, right next to the boy.

The boy wiggled his back as he lay down on the rock that had become warm from the sun.

So did the bear.

The boy opened his arms to feel the sun's warm light on his chest.

So did the bear.

*The boy told the bear to breathe in slowly
through his nose and let the air fill his
stomach like a balloon . . .*

then slowly let the air out through his mouth letting his stomach go down.

The boy put his hands on his belly and felt it get big and round and filled with air.

So did the bear.

Then the boy and the bear together let the air out of their mouths. They both made a gentle aahh sound. The boy liked the way this felt.

So did the bear.

For a few moments they both did this breathing together.

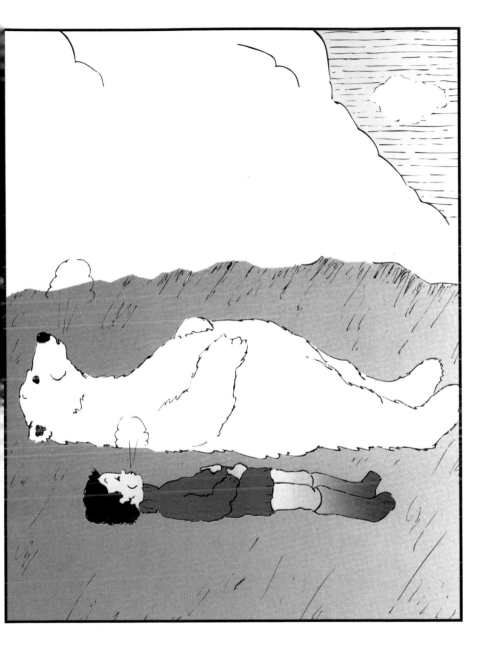

Breathe in 2, 3, 4, out 2, 3, 4, in 2, 3, 4, aahh 2, 3, 4. (Breathe to this count with your child.)

Now the boy was breathing slowly. He felt the sun warming his face and neck. He kept breathing in 2, 3, 4, out 2, 3, 4, in 2, 3, 4, out 2, 3, 4.

So did the bear.

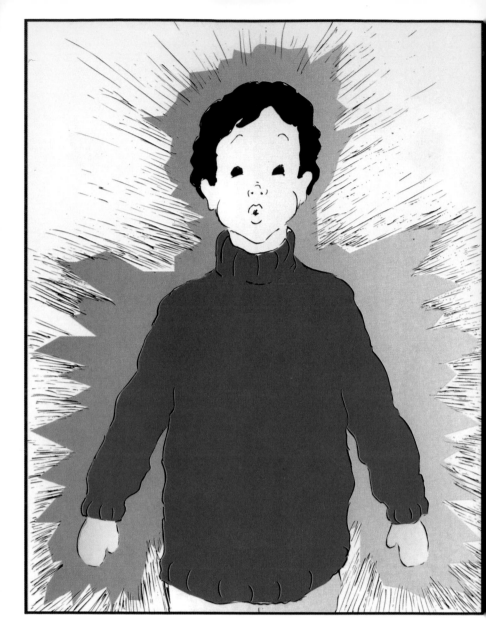

Next the boy felt the sun warming and relaxing his arms.

Then he felt the sun warming and relaxing his legs. So did the bear.

The boy kept breathing slowly. He loved how the sun felt on his belly as it went up and down.

So did the bear

The boy welcomed a big gentle yawn.

So did the bear.

Now every muscle in the boy's body was warm and relaxed and still. The boy felt his eyes close softly as he fell fast asleep.

And so did the bear.